Cinderella

and the prince!

For Samuel, Martha, and Lilly

Text copyright © 2015 by Nosy Crow
Illustrations copyright © 2011 by Nosy Crow
Nosy Crow and its logos are trademarks of Nosy Crow Ltd. Used under license.

First U.S. edition 2016

Library of Congress Catalog Card Number 2015940252
ISBN 978-0-7636-8654-3

15 16 17 18 19 20 GBL 10 9 8 7 6 5 4 3 2 1

Printed in Shenzhen, Guangdong, China

This book was typeset in Clarendon.
The illustrations were created digitally.

Nosy Crow
an imprint of
Candlewick Press
99 Dover Street
Somerville, Massachusetts 02144

www.nosycrow.com
www.candlewick.com

Cinderella

illustrated by Ed Bryan

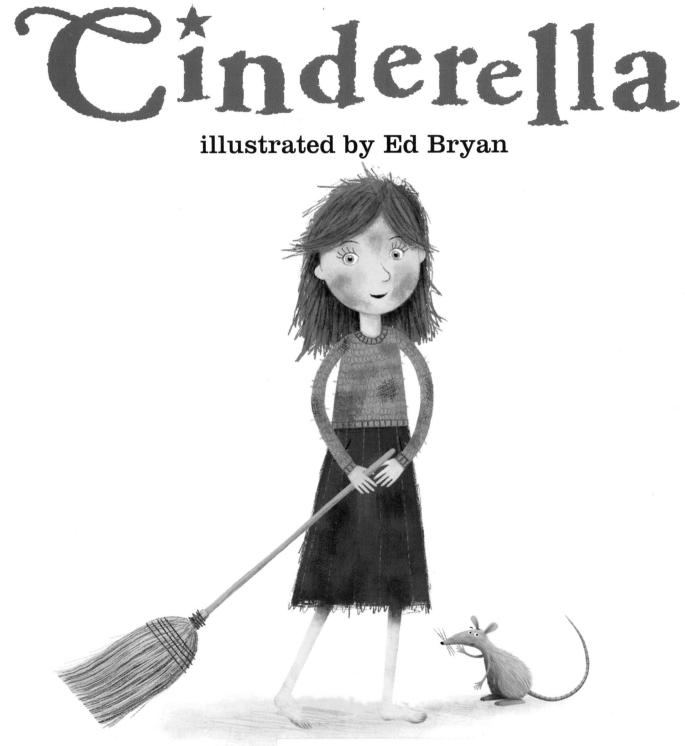

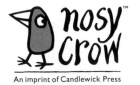

nosy crow™

An imprint of Candlewick Press

Once upon a time, there was a
kind girl called **Cinderella**.

Cinderella had to clean the house all day long, so she had no nice clothes and was always covered in **dust** and **dirt**.

But worst of all, Cinderella lived with her stepmother and stepsisters, who were very mean to her.

Cinderella lived in a country ruled by a **king**, and that king had a **son** who was a kind prince.

"It's time you got married," said the king. "I'll host a **grand ball** so you can meet all the young ladies in the land."

The next day, an **invitation**
arrived at Cinderella's house.

--To the ladies of the house--
the King invites you to a

Royal Ball

with dancing and ice cream
at the palace.
°o°

Please wear your very finest ball gown.

Cinderella's stepmother and stepsisters were all very **excited**. "The prince is **sure** to fall in love with **one** of you!" said the stepmother.

They made **SO** much **noise** that Cinderella came in from the kitchen. "May **I** go to the ball?" she asked.

"Don't be silly, Cinderella. The prince would **never marry you!**" said her stepmother.

On the night of the ball, Cinderella had
to help her stepsisters get ready.

"Fetch my tiara!"
shrieked one stepsister.

"Find my **hair ribbon!**" shouted the other.

After everyone had left to go to the palace, Cinderella cried and cried because she really wanted to go to the ball, too.

As Cinderella sobbed by the fire, a friendly-looking lady **suddenly** appeared.

"I am your fairy godmother," she said. "I am here to make your dream come **true**. Come with me!"

Out in the moonlit garden, the fairy godmother quickly got to work. "We need three **mice** and a **pumpkin**."

With a wave of her wand, the fairy godmother turned the pumpkin into a beautiful **carriage.** Two mice became prancing **horses,** and the third mouse became a **coachman.**

Cinderella's ragged clothes
became a beautiful **ball gown**,
and glass **slippers** appeared
on her feet.

As she left for the palace, Cinderella's fairy godmother gave her a warning. "The magic only lasts until midnight," she said. "You **must** be home by then!"

When Cinderella entered the ballroom, **everyone** turned to look at her.

"She looks familiar," said the stepsisters. "I'm **sure** we've seen her somewhere before."

Right away, the prince asked Cinderella to dance.

Cinderella and the prince danced **all** night long.

But when the clock struck **midnight**, Cinderella remembered her fairy godmother's warning.

"Oh, no," cried Cinderella. "I must go!"

DONG!
DONG!

As Cinderella ran from the ballroom,
one of her glass slippers **fell off.**

The prince picked it up.
"I will marry the girl whose foot fits
this shoe," he said.

Moments later, Cinderella's carriage turned back into a **pumpkin** and the horses and coachman became **mice** again. Cinderella found herself wearing her **ragged clothes** once more.

The prince searched
for Cinderella for
weeks and months.

At last, he arrived at Cinderella's house.
Her stepsisters tried to **push** their feet into
the glass slipper, but they did **not** fit.

Then **Cinderella** looked in from the kitchen. "Would you please bring the shoe over here so I can try it on?" she said.

Cinderella's foot slid easily into the slipper.

"It's a **perfect** fit," she said.
"**I knew** I'd find you in the end!" cried the prince.

The prince and Cinderella had a **wonderful** wedding. Even Cinderella's stepmother and stepsisters were invited.

And Cinderella and the prince lived
happily ever after.

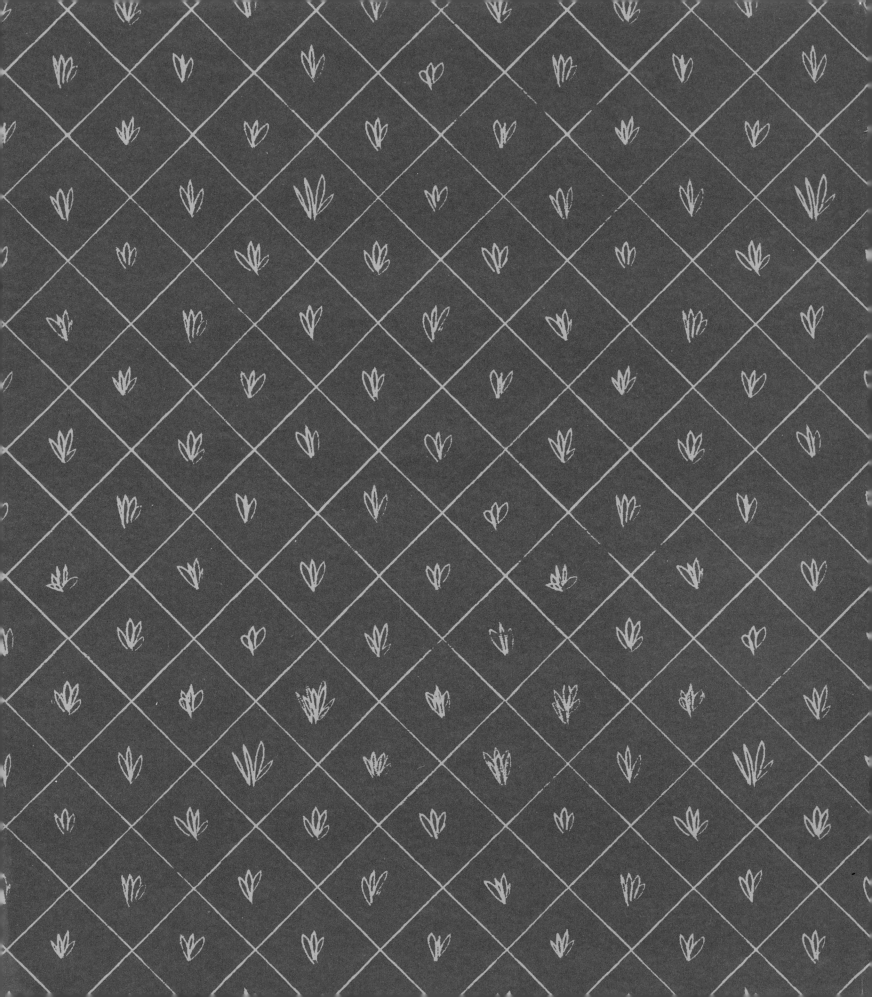